Phoenix Rising:

FLINT RANCH

prelude to a thriller

a novella by

Jette Harris

Moran Publishing

ISBN-13: 978-0692686027
ISBN-10: 0692686029

http://jetterfly.wordpress.com

www.stephenjohnmoran.com

January, 1968

Age 6

The cold air cut into his bones and the frost bit at his bare feet, but Thatch was oblivious. Even the physical pain from the event had faded enough to be overshadowed by the tight betrayal in his chest and burning shame on his face. He ran to the only place within running distance: the stable.

All he wanted was to help his mother. Uncle Jed had no right to drag her by the hair, even a six-year-old knew that. It wasn't right, what he was doing. He hit her so hard, she stopped moving. Tears began to flood over his face again, freezing to his cheeks in the cold Colorado air. Thatch was only trying to help, and it worked; Jed decided to hit him instead, to hold him down and... and... It wasn't right, what he'd done. Thatch didn't know why it was wrong, but he felt it in his heart. And it hurt.

Dread filled him as he pushed open the stable doors. He had never been there after dark. What if Jed came after him? The horses, bedded down for the night, looked up with curiosity. The musky smell of horse abated his panic, and he slid the door shut behind him. The cold was still unbearable inside. He would be dead soon if he didn't find warmth. He was still wearing his funeral clothes, the black slacks now torn. He had been struggling with the tiny

1

buttons on the sleeve of his dress shirt when he heard his mother scream.

Passing several stalls, he found the one he wanted and climbed the gate. Cassie, swollen with foal, lay on the ground. She shook her head as if to ask the little human what it was doing there at such an unusual time. He curled against her, tucking his frozen toes under her belly, stealing her warmth. She flinched at the cold touch, but nuzzled him with her velvet nose, wiping his tears away. Running his fingers into her mane, he pressed his face against her neck and sobbed.

October

Thatch descended the stairs as quietly as he could. He knew just where to step—right next to the wall—to avoid creaking. At the bottom, he leaned forward and peered around the wall, into the dining room. It had never been used for dining, as far as he could remember, but served as his uncle's office. Papers and ledgers were spread across the huge table, along with catalogues, newspapers, and samples of blankets and feed. Jed Flint sat in the middle, his towering stature hunkered over an open ledger.

On his tip-toes, Thatch stepped down and scurried in the opposite direction, through the living room and into the kitchen. The dining room had kitchen access as well, but a heavy swinging door muffled any noise. Judy Adams stood at the sink in a plain denim dress, her ash blonde hair up in a loose bun. It threatened to fall out over her shoulders as she scrubbed dishes.

He pattered up and threw his arms around her legs, hugging them tightly. She twisted with a gasp. Finding her son, she put her hands over her mouth, then pressed them to her heart as she glanced at the dining room door. After confirming they were alone, she smiled down at him and ran a hand over his scalp, drawing her fingers over the hair on the back of his head.

"I came to help you." He grabbed a step-stool and carried it to the edge of the counter.

"Sweetheart, you don't have to–"

"I want to." He was not about to give her an opportunity to refuse. On the stool, his head came just above her shoulder. Judy smiled, but her eyes were sad. She turned to stare at the dish water, then sniffled and handed him a towel.

"I'll wash–you dry."

She rinsed the suds off the plate she had been scrubbing and passed it to Thatch. The warm ceramic felt pleasant in the chilly air. He took his time wiping it with the towel before he placed it in the rack and accepted another one. They worked in silence for several minutes. Judy's smile disappeared, and her throat moved as if she were having trouble swallowing. A lump rose in Thatch's throat as well. Jed rarely left them alone together; Judy was usually busy cleaning the house and yard. Thatch had to

3

steal moments like these while she worked. He opened his mouth several times, but words would not come out.

"What is it, sweetheart?" she asked after the third time he did this. He didn't realize she had seen. He ran a hand up and down his nose and finished drying the formally-clean plate he had been holding to buy himself a second to collect his courage.

"Mama..." he asked, "is Uncle Jed my daddy?"

Judy dropped the plate in her hands and flinched as it disappeared into the sink, splashing them both. "Heavens, no!" she cried, then dropped her voice to a whisper. "Why would you ask such a horrible thing?"

Thatch's face flushed. Tears rose in his throat. He fought to swallow them down. "M–Miss Tuttle asked, the bus driver." He sniffled, but the tears did not come. "I told her I didn't know; I always just call him 'Uncle Jed.'"

"Oh!" Judy huffed, covering her face with wet hands.

"Mama, if Jed's not my daddy, who is?"

She shook her head.

"Have I ever met him?"

Judy took a deep breath and dropped her hands to the counter. "No, sweetie, you've never met him." She sniffled. "Last time I saw him was before you were born, before I came here."

"What's his name?"

A small smile played on her lips, making Thatch's dread melt away. "Wren," she said, "like the bird."

"What's he look like?"

"Very handsome." Her eyes drifted to the clear blue sky over the curtain in front of her. "Very smart. I guess…" She turned to him with a broad, sad-eyed smile. "…you look just like him." She tapped his nose with a soapy finger.

Thatch beamed. He leaned closer, rising on his toes. "You should call him," he whispered. "He can come get us."

Judy frowned. She sniffled again. "It's not as simple as that, Thatch." The dreamy tone disappeared. She picked up another plate and her sponge.

Thatch's eyes filled with tears as his hope was ripped away. "Why not?" His voice waivered.

"It's–It's complicated." She closed her eyes and tilted her head back.

"He'll understand!" Hot tears began to run down his cheeks. "He'll understand, and he'll come take us away. He can save–"

"Your daddy can't save you, boy." A plate slipped away from them and shattered on the floor, punctuating Jed's words. He stood at the mouth of the kitchen, his eyes on the mess of shards at Judy's feet. They stared, waiting, scared out of their tears. "He's a doctor, huh?"

Judy nodded hesitantly. She flinched as he walked into the kitchen, although he moved slowly.

"You know what that means, right, boy?"

Thatch knew *what* a doctor was, but for some reason he didn't think that was what his uncle was asking. Fortunately, Jed continued without waiting for a response.

"It means he's weak. He don't know nothin' but how to read books… and knock up seventeen-year-olds, huh?" His hand shot out and grasped between Judy's legs through her dress. She jumped back against the counter with a cry.

"Stop it!" Thatch shoved Jed's arm away, making the stool tilt forward and clap back down.

Jed grabbed his arm and squeezed until he whimpered. "Boy, I would crush your daddy." His eyes flickered over the boy's body. He lowered his voice. "I'd do him like I do you."

Judy opened her mouth to protest, but Jed raised the back of his hand to her. She snapped her mouth shut and cowered. Thatch's face burned. His shoulders shook with silent sobs. He jerked his arm in attempt to escape. Jed furrowed his brow and released him. Thatch almost stumbled off his stool, but caught himself on the counter. Jed grabbed his other arm and squeezed, his fingers probing the muscle. His bottom jaw jutted out like whenever he was making calculations. Thatch was able to jerk his arm away this time.

"Huh… Go get your boots on, boy. You'll be workin' with me from now on."

Despite the fear he had felt seconds ago, Thatch's heart bounded with joy. "Really?" Jed had never allowed him to help–or even watch–as he and the ranch hands worked. He didn't seem to know about Thatch's late-night retreats to the stable (even though he woke to horses with braided tails and manes). The thought of spending all day around his four-legged friends and doing something important made Thatch's heart swell.

"Jed, no!" Judy protested. "He's far too small."

Thatch's heart broke twice: once at his mother's words, then again at the loud *smack!* as Jed slapped her. She staggered back, pressing a hand over her nose and mouth. Blood seeped through her fingers.

Jed grabbed the front of her dress and pulled her close to growl: "Don't you think I'm a better judge of how *big* or *small* the boy is, huh?"

Thatch's face burned again as he remembered his uncle's massive body pressed against his. He felt so small on those nights…

"He's a growing boy," Jed said louder, shoving Judy away, against the counter. "And growing boys"– Thatch flinched as Jed reached a hand out, but he just ruffled the boy's hair–"need men's work. Not… dishes."

7

He reached into the sink and flicked water on her, then went to the back door.

Thatch stared at his mother. Blood ran between her fingers, down her arm, and over her chin, down her neck. It blossomed dark brown on the collar of her dress. She did not move, standing with her eyes closed.

"Boots, boy!" Jed shouted, making them both jump.

Taking a deep breath, Thatch stepped down off the stool. He pressed the towel to her free hand as he passed. She wrapped her hand around his fingers. They slipped away as he followed his uncle to the back door, where his barely-used work boots were waiting.

The room was too dark for Thatch to see. When a large hand pressed onto his back, shaking him, he rolled over with a cry.

"Hob yer lip, boy. Wake up, it's time for work."

"It's still dark," Thatch mumbled. He pulled his thin wool blanket back up to his chin.

"What are you, now, a rooster?" Jed grabbed the boy by the back of his neck and lifted him from the bed. Thatch groaned. His muscles were sore and stiff from the unfamiliar labor the day before. "Wake yourself up, boy, before I think of another way to wake you, huh?"

"Like coffee?" Thatch asked, rubbing his eyes.

Jed released a growling sigh as he left the room. Thatch pulled the door to, but it drifted open a few inches. His doorknob had gone missing soon after Aunt Betty's funeral, leaving a gaping hole in the door. Thatch dressed quickly, before his uncle felt compelled to come back.

The rich smell of strong coffee had his brain buzzing as he stepped into the kitchen. By the time he usually woke up, the smell had dissipated enough to be a faint memory hanging around the grounds in the trash can.

"You didn't finish your breakfast. Is something wrong with it?"

Thatch padded up to the threshold, still in his socks. Judy was standing by the stove with a plate in her hand, her eyes wide with concern. His uncle was sitting by the back door, tying his work boots, a piece of bacon slowly disappearing into his mouth. He glanced up and nodded toward the boy. When Judy followed the gesture, her mouth fell open.

"What are you doing up before the sun?" Thatch asked. He pressed his face against his mother's body and wrapped his arms around her legs. The smoky smell of bacon made his stomach contract with hunger.

Wide-eyed, Judy looked from the boy to Jed, her mouth flapping. He answered her by clomping down one boot and proceeding to tie the other.

"I'm–I'm making breakfast, sweetheart," she finally said. She took a fork and spread the remains from Jed's plate until it resembled an entire portion. She extracted herself from the boy's arms and placed the plate on the table.

"Eat fast," Jed said. "You got two hours."

Judy narrowed her eyes at him. He narrowed his eyes right back before pushing through the back door.

"Two hours is a long time." Thatch smiled up at his mother as he took a seat.

"Not when you're working, sweetheart." She sank into the chair next to his.

Thatch relished eating the bacon, eggs, and toast. His usual breakfast before running to the bus was a bowl of oatmeal or cereal. Judy stared at the table, her eyes out of focus, her fingers running through the hair at the back of Thatch's head. He wanted to eat slowly, savoring this absent-minded attention, but the food disappeared quickly. When Judy noticed his clean plate, she gave him a smile that didn't reach her eyes.

"Have a nice day at work," she joked, kissing his forehead.

The shovel was heavy. The stables were cold. Having the horses nearby stopped being a source of comfort when Thatch's hands grew chapped. His palms began to crack and blister. Jed had walked him through how to muck out the first stall. Between the two of them, it had been quick and easy. But now his uncle had disappeared, and pushing the shovel was not as easy with two hands as it had been with four.

Thatch fought to hold back his tears, but when the first blister burst and oozed pus across his palm, they began to stream down his face. Not wanting to disappoint his uncle, he continued to push the shovel despite the pain, his shoulders shaking.

"Why you cryin', huh?" Jed asked, returning with a bale of hay over each shoulder. He thumped them down on each side of the stable.

A sob escaped Thatch's throat. He swallowed and spread his hands.

The corners of Jed's mouth turned down. "Oh, that's nothin'." He ran his hand over the boy's face in a half-hearted attempt to wipe the tears away. "Those'll go away in a few days. I'll find you some gloves for this afternoon."

"Thatch!" Judy called from the back porch. "Your bus–you have ten minutes!"

Ten minutes? What happened to two hours? Dropping the shovel, Thatch shot toward the gate. Jed stopped him with a hand through his collar and pulled him back.

"He's not done yet!" Jed bellowed.

His harsh tone made Thatch's eyes widen with fear. He didn't like that tone; It usually meant other things. He ducked out of his uncle's grip and backed away. The horses didn't like it either, snorting and stamping.

"What, huh?" Jed lumbered past him, back to the bales. Thatch shook his head. "C'mon, boy. Lemme show you how to drop a bale."

"He's late!" Judy hissed with her hands on her hips as they mounted the porch stairs.

Jed was unruffled. "I'll drop him off on my way to town. Get your bag, boy."

Thatch shot past him and into the back door. Being able to feed his friends eased his pain and cheered him up.

"He can't go to school dressed like that! He's covered in—in mud!"

"I'm leavin' now." Jed stood on the top step so he was face-to-face with her. Judy was tall, for a woman. Betty, her older sister, had been slightly taller, and much more gullible until Judy came along with her bouncing baby.

Judy lowered her gaze and ran her hands over the front of her skirt. "I can take him after he changes."

Jed barked a laugh. "Oh, the little rich girl knows how to drive a truck!" He leaned close to her face with a shark-like grin. "Uh-uh. No. Huh? You're not goin' anywhere with him." He turned and clomped back down the stairs. "C'mon, boy!"

Slope's Valley Elementary School was in town, over half an hour from Flint Hill. When Thatch first started school, the bus didn't come out that far. But when Jed was threatened by the truancy officer for the amount of days Thatch had been late and absent, he used his family influence to get Flint Ranch added to the bus route. It didn't make much sense to Thatch, seeing as he was the only kid out there, but he didn't question it: Unless he was truly ill, the days he spent home from school had been unpleasant.

Jed pulled his battered blue pick-up to the curb in front of the school just as the bell rang. The children loitering around the entrance stampeded inside. Thatch pushed his door open, but Jed grabbed his book bag and pulled him back in. He hadn't said anything for the entire drive. This sudden interest startled Thatch.

"Listen, boy…" He dropped his voice low. "You tell anyone about how we play?"

Thatch's face burned. He never knew telling was something he could do: He didn't have many friends, and, although the teachers were nice enough, the thought of telling them what happened at bedtime upset his stomach. If he opened his mouth to reply, he feared he would begin to cry again. He shook his head instead.

"Because, you know…" Jed cleared his throat and donned a sympathetic tone. "… if anyone were to find out– even one person–your mama could get in a lot of trouble, don't cha know, for lettin' it happen an' all."

Thatch's throat grew tight. He wanted to protest she didn't *let* it happen; Jed hit her when she tried to help. He lowered his head as if waiting for this retort, but Thatch held it in.

"If anyone finds out, you just might never see your mama again. Remember that."

A strangled whimper escaped Thatch's throat. He looked to the school, for anyone who might be able to see, and know, and help, but there were only children running away from them.

"So, don't tell anyone, huh?"

Thatch nodded rapidly. Jed reached out. Thatch recoiled against the door. His uncle's grip on his bag prevented him from escaping, but he only mussed his hair with a lop-sided grin.

"I'll see you after school, then."

Thatch jumped out of the truck and ran inside, his book bag flopping against his back. He flew down the hallway and into the door of his second-grade classroom. Just as the bell rang, he skidded to a halt by his desk. He panted to catch his breath.

Everything about the ranch–even his uncle's truck– smelled of horse. He hadn't thought anything of it; The smell brought him comfort. But now, in the middle of the classroom that usually smelled of children and chalk dust, the rich, warm smell of manure filled his nose. He looked down. His throat grew tight: He was still wearing his work boots, wet and caked with manure. They had left a trail of mucky water from the door–and possibly all the way down the hall. His jeans, which were two inches too short, were wet up to the knee and brown stains almost reached as high.

Holding his breath, Thatch glanced around without raising his head. Everyone was staring, even the teacher. Their faces were twisted in disgust at the scent he loved so much.

"Mrs. White," a girl cried, "Thatch smells like *shit!*"

The class burst into laughter. Thatch began to tremble and choke. He turned and ran out of the classroom. The laughter followed him down the empty hallway, and tears streamed down his face.

April, 1969

Age 7

Thatch's hands developed thick callouses. He learned exactly what time he had to be out of bed, how long it took to muck out the stalls and drop bales, and to lay out his school clothes the night before, so he could change and run out the door just in time to catch the bus. By his seventh birthday, he had it down to an art; He didn't want Jed pulling him out of bed every morning.

Some mornings he would come in early.

The days were just starting to warm up, requiring a heavy coat in the morning and a light shirt in the afternoon. Thatch placed a stool in the sunlight flooding in through the stable doors. Archie, Cassie's foal, played with Thatch's hair as he cleaned the mare's hoof with a stiff brush.

"Not using a knife, huh?"

Jed's voice made Thatch jump and knock Archie's nose with his head. "I don't want to hurt her," he replied, stroking the colt's nose apologetically.

"You won't." He clutched two rifles by their barrels. One was Jed's old Enfield. The other was newer. Thatch had never seen it before.

16

"She started bleeding last time." Realizing he was arguing, he conceded with a shrug. "Besides, I'm much better with a brush."

Jed snorted. He caught the boy eyeing the rifles with interest and rested their butts on the ground. "Almost done?"

"With Cassie." Thatch turned his attention back to the hoof in his hand. "Goldie's next."

Jed passed Goldie's stall, leaning down to inspect her hooves. "She can wait, huh," he said. He pulled a blanket from the shelf and threw it over his shoulder. "Finish up and put those two away."

He grabbed a coffee can containing used-but-maybe-still-good nails and rattled them around the bottom. Archie shook his head and snorted at the unpleasant noise. Jed dumped the nails into an old toolbox, then placed the can upside-down on Thatch's head as he walked out.

"C'mon, boy," he said. "We're losing light."

The can fell down over Thatch's eyes. He pushed it back up on his head. Checking Cassie's remaining hoof for pebbles, he dislodged a clump of dirt with a finger and led the horses back into their stall. The coffee can bounced painfully against his scalp as he hurried after his uncle, but he did not remove it.

Jed walked to the fence, then took ten broad strides back toward Thatch. When he stopped, he laid the blanket out across the grass and set the rifles down on each end.

Reaching into his pocket, he pulled out a handful of rounds. He rolled them across his palm and tossed them by their respective rifles. Thatch stood behind his uncle, holding his breath. His heart bounded with fear and excitement. Either Jed was about to shoot him, or teach him how to shoot.

"Did…" Thatch swallowed hard. "Did you buy a new rifle, Uncle Jed?"

Jed lifted the coffee can from Thatch's head. "Won it off Virgil's cousin. Said he never wanted to see it again, anyway." He turned the can and tapped on the white "C" of *Coffee*, the largest letter on the label. "Keep your eye on that."

As Jed walked to the fence to place the can on a post, an image flit through Thatch's mind of his uncle lying face-down in the grass. He eyed the rounds and rifles on the ground, trying to divine how to put them together… But he couldn't do that, even if he knew how to: Police would come. He would go to jail. Mama could get in trouble, or worse. Jed had made all of that clear a long time ago.

Jed taught Thatch all the parts of a rifle and told him their names. He showed him how to load the clip, and helped when the boy's fingers weren't strong enough. He told him the history of the Enfield, used in the War to kill Italians, and the newer rifle was called a modified Springfield M40, but he never elaborated on what the modifications were.

"Is it going to be loud?" Thatch asked as they laid down on their bellies.

"You betcha." Jed peered through the scope, then turned the knob on the side.

"What're you doing?"

"Sighting it in." Jed fell silent again, looking through the scope, then at the trees, then turning the knob on the top.

"What's that mean?" Thatch whispered.

Jed made a noise low in his throat. Thatch fell silent; He only made that noise when he was losing patience. Licking his lips, Thatch pressed his eye to the scope. At first he couldn't see anything. Frowning, he shifted until the trees beyond the fence loomed close. Blinking, he found the coffee can and shifted again until the "C" was between the crosshairs.

"Will you need to—"

With an ear-splitting *BOOM!* the rifle bucked against his shoulder. Jed jumped back with a shout. Thatch lay frozen, mouth hanging open. Dull pain radiated through his shoulder. He closed his mouth and squeezed his eyes shut, fighting, but his body began to shudder with sobs. He whimpered as tears escaped down his cheeks.

"Hob your lip, boy." Jed settled back down. "Cryin's for girls, don't cha know? You're not a girl, are you, huh?" He pressed his eye back against the scope and muttered, "I think I woulda noticed that."

19

Thatch lowered his face, inhaling the residual smell of horses. He clutched the blanket and wiped his tears away. His racing heart slowed.

"At least the bullet wasn't wasted."

Blinking with surprise, Thatch raised his head. Jed nodded toward the fence. The coffee can rocked on the ground. Smiling, Thatch turned to his uncle, but Jed scowled.

"Took me two goddamn months to hit a can, and you go and hit it by accident first shot..." he muttered. He reached over and pulled the clip from Thatch's rifle. Taking the M40 and Thatch's ammunition, retrieved the can from the ground, and shook his head at it. Thatch bit his lip. When Jed slammed the can back onto the post, Thatch placed his eye to the scope.

"Just a lucky shot!" Jed yelled as he trudged back.

Thatch found the can, but didn't see any holes in the red label. "I don't see it."

"Look at the 'o,'" Jed grunted as he lowered himself back onto the ground.

Then Thatch saw it: He had blown a hole through the middle of the 'o,' less than an inch from where he had been aiming. His eyes went wide. "Wow..." He turned to Jed, hoping to see a smile, but his uncle continued to scowl and would not look at him.

"Like I said, beginner's luck. You weren't even aimin', huh." He tossed the clip back over to Thatch's side of the blanket.

"Can I go again?" Thatch's heart was racing again, now the shock had passed. Jed's skepticism did little to dampen his spirits. Thatch smiled so wide, it hurt his cheeks. Maybe his uncle would be impressed if he hit the "C" like he was supposed to.

Jed studied his nephew's smiling face. He made the low noise in his throat again. "Hold your horses, boy."

The sun sank low, and the air grew chilly. Thatch pulled his arms close to his chest and propped his chin where he could watch the can through his scope as Jed emptied his clip at it. He hit it twice: grazing it once, and hitting below the lip on his last round. By the time he returned from perching it back on the fencepost, stars dotted the purple sky.

"Is it my turn?" Thatch asked, smiling up at his uncle.

"Too dark," Jed grunted. He bent down and picked up his rifle.

Thatch's heart sank. His smile disappeared. "But–"

Jed rounded on him. "But what, boy? I said it was too dark!" Rifle over his shoulder, he turned back toward the house.

"That's not fair!" Thatch jumped to his feet. "I thought we were taking turns!"

Jed cleared his throat. At least, that's what it sounded like at first. Thatch's face fell when he realized his uncle was laughing at him. Jed turned to him slowly. Thatch swallowed. He backed away, then dove for the rifle.

January, 1970

Age 8

Footsteps thudded up the stairs. Thatch's hands shook. He fought to lie still, obedient, but his courage failed him. He slipped out from under the sheets, his naked skin prickling with goosebumps. He pulled on his threadbare flannel pajamas, but they did little to alleviate the biting cold. He held his breath as the footsteps passed his door. Jed would spend a few minutes in his room, undressing, getting ready. He preferred to walk in naked and fully-erect.

Thatch had tried hiding under the bed, in the closet, and behind the dresser, only to be dragged out and thrown onto the bed, or crushed into the hardwood floor. Escaping the room through the door was out of the question; Jed left his door open as he prepared. Thatch's breath came in ragged gasps. His heart pounded against his ribs.

Frost was already creeping up the window pane, although the sun set less than an hour ago. He pulled on some wooly socks, then eased the window up. He had greased the tracks with shortening. Judy had pretended she didn't see him take it; She overlooked most of the things her son did these days. She would swallow as if her throat was tight and turn away. Thatch used to do things to get a rise out of her. He stopped after he broke a plate, and when Jed demanded what happened, she took responsibility. Judy could not see through her left eye for three days.

The window rose smoothly and quietly. The cold bit at Thatch's face and fingers as he eased himself out onto the roof. Although Jed forced him out there last autumn to clean the gutters, the fear of falling through a weak spot right into the living room was paralyzing. His hands shook from fear–not cold–as he slid the window back down. Backing against the side of the house, he tucked his feet under his body and waited.

From this side of the roof, Thatch could see the end of the stable. Swallowing, he tried to focus on remembering the patterns on his favorite horse, Archie. Heavy footsteps approached within the house, and Thatch's door groaned open. His face burned. *Horses* didn't feel shame. He wished he could be more like a horse: hard-working and impervious, independent. Cloth rustled as Jed threw the sheets back. He grunted. Thatch took a deep breath and held it. He was tempted to peer inside as he heard wood scraping and the closet door squeaking, but he was too terrified to move. He kept his eyes fixed on the stable.

"Where are you, huh?" Jed asked in a low voice.

Thatch's head began to swim as he ran out of air. His chest grew sore, but he was too scared to breathe. Jed released a long, growling sigh. His heavy steps faded as he left the room. Thatch dared to breathe, but not to move. As soon as Jed's door closed, he would crawl back inside and curl up to sleep under the bed.

A scream tore through the house. Thatch cried out. Throwing open the window, he fell inside. All of his weight came down on his wrist with a crunch. He slumped onto his side and opened his mouth in a breathless howl. Judy screamed again. Hot tears streamed down his face as he scrambled to his feet and shot out of the room. He collided with his mother's door. It flew open, depositing him once more onto the floor.

Jed Flint was on his sister-in-law's bed, straddling her legs. He tore at her pajamas with one hand, while pinning her hands with the other. Jed jerked his head up.

"No!" Judy wailed. Her body fell still. She turned her face away.

"I'm here!" Thatch threw himself at his uncle. His fists were pathetic as he beat at his uncle's rock-hard shoulder. "I'm here! Leave her alone!"

Jed stepped off the bed. Judy clawed at his torso as he scooped the boy up and tucked him under his arm. Crying bitterly, Thatch resigned himself as Jed carried him toward the door.

"Put him down!" cried Judy, grabbing Jed's free arm.

Twisting, Jed shoved her to the floor. She pushed herself back up. He raised a foot and slammed it into her stomach. She collapsed into a heap, gasping for air, but struggled to her feet again.

"Stay down!" he roared. Wrapping a brawny hand around Thatch's throat, he dangled the boy over his mother. Judy's knees buckled. She reached out in a hopeless attempt to support Thatch's feet, then pressed her hands to her mouth.

Gasping for air, Thatch clawed at Jed's hands. Acid welled up from his stomach. The blood that could not escape his head pounded in his brain. His body grew heavy. He wanted nothing more than to fall still and allow sleep to take him. His mother, shaking with sobs, lowered her face to the floor, hands out in supplication.

Jed snorted. He swung the boy back under his arm. Thatch hacked and coughed. His body hung limp. Tears ran down his face. He tried not to sob as Jed dropped him onto his bed and peeled off his pajamas. He clamped his teeth over his bottom lip, but could not suppress a scream as his uncle tore into him. A hand clapped over his face.

"Hob your lip, huh? You're upsettin' your ma. You don't want to upset your ma even more, do you, boy?"

Whimpering, Thatch shook his head. He fell perfectly still. Jed released his face and pushed his head down with a gentle hand. The boy pressed the sheets into his mouth and waited silently for it to end.

June, 1972

Age 10

Jed killed the rabbit. He snatched it from Thatch's hands and twisted its head right off. Thatch's stomach lurched. Judy gaped as Jed handed the limp body to her. The head left a trail of blood across the kitchen floor as he carried it to the trash can. Thatch was afraid he was going to be sick, or worse, cry. Last time he cried outside of the bedroom, his uncle cuffed him and said he would show him a man. Thatch found this amusing, since his manhood was now about as big as his uncle's.

Thatch swallowed the vomit and held his breath until he was out the back door. He should have known better than to bring the thing inside in the first place. He just wanted something to show his mom, to make her talk to him. He should have known it would end up as soup.

"Where you goin' so fast, boy?"

"I need to clip Archie," Thatch muttered as he stumbled down the porch stairs. Jed snickered. Thatch's chest was tight. He could feel his uncle's eyes on his back until he turned into the stable. The musty smell of straw and animal filled his nostrils. His muscles relaxed instantly, all but his tight throat.

Archie nickered and threw his head when he recognized his human. Thatch pulled him out. He could complete the process in quick, mechanical motions. Today he took his time, focusing on each step of saddling to distract him from the lump in his throat. Archie shook his head impatiently, nudging Thatch's face and shoulders whenever he was within reach.

"Stop it," he scolded, pushing on his nose. But he couldn't help smiling. His tight throat loosened. "Stop trying to cheer me up."

Archie side-stepped defiantly, knocking the boy to the ground. Thatch laughed, but choked on it. He glanced at each entrance as he stood and brushed himself off. Finding themselves alone except for the other horses, watching enviously, Thatch took the harness and pressed his forehead to Archie's soft nose. His hugged the horse's neck, breathed in his warmth, and giggled. His giggles turned to sniffles and heaving sobs.

Swallowing, Thatch tightened all the straps, climbed on a railing, and pulled himself up into the saddle. As soon as Archie was free of the stable door, Thatch clicked his tongue twice. The horse flew into a gallop.

The urge to cry faded as Thatch focused on his footing and the ground sloping ahead of them. The sharp wind dried his tears into salty trails. He didn't rein Archie at all; He didn't need to. Although he would have allowed the horse to wander anywhere he wished, Archie knew where his boy wanted to go. He galloped across the property, over half a mile, until they reached the fence.

Archie cantered along the perimeter until they both heard it: A drift of distant music, rock 'n' roll blaring from a neighboring property.

Flint Ranch didn't have a TV or radio. The only music Thatch had been exposed to was at school and in stores the few times he had gone into town. A few months ago, one of the ranch hands, Virgil, convinced Jed to let Thatch accompany him and his daughter on a trip to the Feed 'n' Seed. The oddest-sounding music was coming from the radio. Virgil called it Ziggy Stardust. Thatch held his breath as he listened to the words. They had tugged at something bittersweet in his chest, something he ached for once it had gone.

When Thatch heard the music through the woods, although it was very different from the Ziggy Stardust, he felt the tug in his chest again. It comforted him too much; Music was not forbidden at Flint Ranch, but riding out to listen to it felt like an act of rebellion. Thatch dreaded Jed going to the neighbors and burning down their house, or at least threatening them if they don't turn down the music.

At the same time, the music and this small act of defiance were sources of rare pleasure. Archie stopped where the music was clearest, and Thatch dismounted. He reached into the saddlebag and pulled out an old, tattered copy of *Huckleberry Finn*. He laid down on the grass with an arm behind his head, only to have Archie attempt to lie on top of him. Laughing, he leaned and scooted until he made the horse his pillow.

Clouds drifted across the clear, blue sky. Music drifted through the trees. Thatch cracked open the book and drifted down the Mississippi River with a large Black man, both escapees.

For a few stolen hours, his pain was far away.

April, 1973

Age 11

The hinges squeaked as Thatch opened the bedroom door. The sound was barely audible, but to Thatch it was as loud as a siren, alerting his uncle of the intruder. He froze, his hand on the doorknob, straining to listen, but the house was empty; Jed was breaking a new horse, and his mother was washing linens. He eased the door open, just wide enough for him to slip inside.

Jed's room was cold and smelled like the inside of an old leather boot. Judy had already gathered the dirty laundry from the floor. Jed never spent enough time awake in his own room to make a mess, although he never hesitated to make a mess of his nephew's. Thatch glanced around, searching for something that would not be missed. He had already stolen a pair of boots he had never seen Jed wear, a vase that only held dead stems, and an antique spittoon that had never been cleaned out.

Thatch pulled back the curtain to peer out the window. He had a perfect view of his mother hanging sheets on the line. An unidentifiable emotion stirred in his chest, torn between melancholy and anger. She had barely spoken to him for years. Years of silent Sunday dinners, joyless Christmases, bitter birthdays. Why did she have to shut him out like that?

Judy returned to the laundry basket. The other sheets were perfect, pristine, *white*. The fitted sheet she pulled out next was covered in red and brown stains–his sheet. He closed his eyes, face burning with shame. Last night had been especially bad. She had to wash that out and hang it on the line like the flag of some victorious conqueror. A sound drifted up to him. He opened his eyes to see his mother, face pressed into the sheet, drop to her knees. Linens forgotten, she bowed to the ground and sobbed.

Thatch swallowed the lump in his throat and wiped away some tears. His chest was tight. Taking a deep breath, he glanced around. His eyes landed on a framed black-and-white photo on top of the dresser. Jed and Aunt Betty, dressed in their wedding finery, smiled fixedly at him. Thatch clenched his teeth. Surely Jed would miss it, but Thatch didn't care: It would be in pieces and buried by the time he noticed.

Rising on his toes, Thatch snatched it from the dresser, leaving an outline in the thick dust. He spun toward the door, but froze mid-step. His heart pounded against his ribs. Jed stood in the doorway. His cold grey eyes stared down his nose at the boy. His jaw clenched and unclenched, but his face remained expressionless. He took a deep breath.

"Where you goin' with that–*boy*?"

Thatch could not move, breathe, or think. He attempted to answer, but his mouth would not cooperate. His muscles were twisted and tense.

"I asked you a question." Jed took a step toward him. Every fiber in Thatch's body screamed for him to run, but there was nowhere to go. Jed's immense stature filled the doorway. Thatch's ragged breathing finally pulled enough oxygen for his brain to function. He swallowed.

"P–p–plinking."

"What?"

"Pl–plinking. I was gonna use it for–for target practice."

The smile that twisted across Jed's face was more fearsome than any scowl. "Give it here, boy." He held out his hand.

Thatch surrendered it, trying not to get too close, but Jed grabbed his wrist, crushing and twisting, before taking the frame. Thatch fought a child-like cry. Jed scrutinized the photo as if he had never seen it before. Given the amount of dust on it, that was possible.

"So, you're telling me, you were gonna use my face for target practice, huh?"

"Yes." Thatch's voice trembled with tears.

"To shoot at?"

"Yes." The word came out firmer this time.

"Do you want to shoot me, boy?"

Anger rose in his throat, overwhelming his fear and springing out of his mouth: "Yes!"

Jed's eyes widened with surprise and flickered over him, then returned to the photo. His gaze fell upon the shiny frame. "And what about the silver, huh?"

"What?"

"The silver frame. What were you gonna do with it?"

"I already told you!"

Jed twisted Thatch's arm. "Do you know how much this is worth?"

"No!"

"You expect me to believe you are gonna shoot at– to destroy–this silver, then just throw it away, huh?"

"Yes!"

Jed swung the frame into Thatch's head. The glass cracked, taking some of his hair as he reeled. He would have fallen were it not for Jed's iron grip on his wrist.

"Stop lyin' to me!"

"I'm not!" The frame hit his head again. The glass shattered, shards cutting into his scalp and raining onto the floor.

"Did that little Red girl put you up to this?" Jed screamed, "Are you fuckin' her, boy?"

"What?" The unfamiliar word jarred Thatch out of his panic enough to process the correct response: "No!"

"Are you still lyin' to me?" Jed threw the broken frame against the wall.

"No!"

Jed slammed his fist into Thatch's head. The boy hit the ground, his skull cracking against the hardwood. His mind grew foggy; He did not want to get up again. Maybe this time, if he didn't move, Jed would stop. Maybe this time...

"Stop it!"

Thatch gasped. Head spinning, he pushed himself up on his elbows to find his mother standing in the doorway. Jed grabbed her by the throat and slammed her into the wall.

"Ma!" Thatch jumped to his feet. The room reeled and lurched, almost sending him back to the floor. His mother was turning purple. Jumping, Thatch threw himself on Jed's back, wrapping his arms around his uncle's thick neck.

Jed tossed Judy aside. Grabbing at the boy's head, he clutched his arm and pulled him loose. He slammed Thatch's body against the wall until he lost his grip. The boy fell, face-down. The floor knocked the remaining breath out of him. Jed grabbed Thatch's hair and began to slam his forehead against the hardwood.

Thatch's view oscillated from his mother to the red stain blooming on the floor under his face. Judy raised her head, her fingers creeping toward him. Thatch's mind went blank before he could reach her.

All Thatch could feel was pressure, against his back and inside of him, the rhythmic pushing and pulling, then a pause. The pressure disappeared as Jed stood. Pulling the straps of his overalls back over his shoulders, he left the room without a word.

Consciousness crept up on him. Thatch didn't know if it was evening or morning, but dusky light filtered in through the curtains. He may have been staring at his door for several hours. It may have been a few minutes. He didn't remember ever seeing it closed before. Beyond it, he could hear a woman sobbing.

Thatch grunted to confirm he was still alive. He attempted to move his head, but his neck was so stiff, he abandoned the idea. He lay on his stomach across his bed. He could not remember how he got there, but flashes of what followed shot through his mind. He squeezed his eyes shut, trying to block them out.

One arm dangled off the edge of the bed. Slowly, he curled and uncurled his fingers. The third finger refused to move, sending searing pain into his knuckle. He attempted to move his other arm from above his head. It was numb.

He dragged it down to his side and sensation returned with fiery pins and needles. When he moved his legs, a tearing sensation shot between them and up his back, making him cry out.

Thatch gave up attempting to move. He began to cry, although the heaving sobs wracked him with pain.

Jed had put a padlock on the door. Once, sometimes twice a day, usually in the morning, he would visit. These visits were Thatch's only method of telling time. He would begin to cry the moment the hasp scraped. He wished for death, that the pain would kill him. It never did.

After Jed thumped downstairs, a mouse-like footfall would scurry to the door. The padlock would shift, but held. Jed was too careful. A red-rimmed blue eye would peer through the hole where the knob should have been. Thatch was in too much pain to move. It was painful enough clutching for the sheet to cover his naked body. All he could do to protect his mother now was close his eyes, force together his cracked lips, and pretend to snore.

A bucket had been placed by the bed for him to use as a toilet. He could barely move, and often reached it too late, or missed it altogether. When Jed visited, he would toss the contents out the window. He never brought food. After peering into Thatch's glassy eyes, he brought a bucket of water and left it on the dresser. Thatch managed to pull himself up and shove his face into the water, lapping it like a dog.

His captivity felt like forever. In reality, it was only six days. Thatch's freedom was uneventful. He hadn't noticed Jed had left the door open until he bellowed up the stairs.

"Boy! Get yer lazy ass outside! The stalls haven't been mucked all week!"

Thatch's eyes shot open. His breath caught in his throat. It had to be a trick.

The horses must be miserable. Thatch clung to this thought. He swallowed his bitterness and fear. Clenching his teeth against the pain, he lowered himself off the edge of the bed, crouching until sure his legs could support his weight.

He tugged his waste-crusted sheets and blanket from the bed and piled them by the door. He was able to pull on a button-up shirt and jeans, but his torso and legs were too sore to bend over and pull on socks. Half-limping, half-dragging himself, he made it downstairs. He stepped into his boots and paused at the back door. Outside, Jed was tossing bales of hay off the bed of his pick-up. Thatch waited, hand on the door knob, for him to finish and move farther away.

A gasp and a thud made him turn. The wrenching motion radiated pain throughout his body, making him see stars. When they cleared, his mother was standing on the threshold of the kitchen, the laundry basket at her feet and a hand over her mouth.

His breath came in ragged gasps. His lips began to tremble. Judy kicked past the basket and pulled him into her arms. His entire body felt bruised and sore, but he clung to her, fighting the urge to cry again.

"Oh, my poor boy," she sobbed. "My baby boy…" She ran her fingers through the hair on the back of his head, and he buried his face against her shoulder. She kissed his forehead above the contusion that spread across it. "I love you," she whispered. "I'm so–"

"–fuck're you doin', huh?" Jed threw open the back door. They sprang apart. "Did you hear me, boy? Get out there and get to work!"

Judy's fingers trailed down his arm. She squeezed his hand before they parted. Jed leered at her, his hand flat as if he were going to raise it to slap her, but he did not. At least, not as Thatch was heading out the door.

Virgil Roanhorse, Flint Ranch's senior ranch hand, leaned on a pitchfork by the stable door. He was a short, sturdy, bronze-faced man who wore his black hair in a braid down his back. He kept a cool demeanor, unless he was cracking one of his rare jokes, but there was shock in his eyes when his gaze fell upon the boy. Thatch kept his face toward the ground as he passed.

"Thatch?"

"I fell off a horse," he lied. No matter what he said, Thatch knew Virgil would know the truth. There was no way he couldn't. Thatch fought to walk properly as he passed the stalls. It brought him no comfort to step inside; The stable smelled rank with mildew and manure.

"What're you doing?" Virgil asked as Thatch reached for the shovel.

"Jed told me to muck out the stalls." Thatch placed a hand on the handle, unsure whether he would be able to wrap his fingers around it.

"No, no, son," Virgil said. "Brush down the horses."

"Jed said–"

"Jed's gone to get feed." He confiscated the shovel and handed Thatch the brush. "He told *me* to tell *you*, *I* will muck out the stalls, and you're to brush down the horses."

Thatch closed his eyes and waited for the tears of gratitude to fade. He couldn't force the words past the lump in his throat, but he mouthed them: "Thank you."

Thatch didn't know when he would be able to ride again. *Never*, his youthful sense of permanence told him, not with the tearing sensation he experienced any time he swung his gait a little too wide. Too sore to go on his own and too injured to ride, he pulled Archie out to lean on. The horse walked extra-slow, pausing occasionally to nibble dandelions so Thatch could rest.

On the far end of the ranch, where no one but horses ever wandered, three posts had been driven into the ground.

Broken glass and rusty cans lay scattered around their bases. An old saddle, worn and flaking, lay on the ground thirty yards in front of them. Thatch sighed with relief when he noticed a small rifle leaning upon it. His trip had not been wasted.

He didn't expect to see anyone when he looked around, but he did so anyway. After a few failed attempts, he whistled a short tune. A small girl materialized out of the woods.

Virginia Roanhorse, two years younger than Thatch, was small and sturdy like her father. Her dark hair looked as if her mother lopped it to the chin with kitchen shears every month or so. She moved silently, her footfalls nothing more than a soft breeze over the grass. When Thatch stepped out from behind of the horse, Ginny's eyes went wide. Her hands flew to her mouth.

"I waited," she said in a small, tight voice. "When I came to see what was taking so long, I heard screaming…"

Thatch lowered his head. "He caught me," he confessed. His lie about falling off a horse would not have worked with her anyway; She knew him too well.

He took Archie to the fence and tied him off. Ginny mercifully did not ask him to elaborate. Seeing her brought the memory back into clear light: Despite what he told Jed, she *had* been part of the reason Thatch had been in his room. A question tugged at his mind as he returned to her. "Ginny, what does *fucken* mean?"

"Fucken," she repeated under her breath. "Oh! *Fucking*! It's a curse word, means to have sex, to fuck."

"Sex?" He heard this word at school, but had only a vague concept of what it meant.

"Rutting. Mating."

"Oh." Thatch blushed. Why would Jed accuse him of doing something like that with her? She was far too young to be useful. As he applied the term to humans, the image in his head fell into place. *Fucking*. That was what Jed was doing, he was *fucking* him. A painful jolt shot through his belly as he imagined himself using her the way Jed used him. Grimacing, he turned and limped toward the old saddle. Now the word made sense: *Fuck*. Short, hard, painful.

"Why?"

"Something Jed said. Don't ask… please."

"Where have you been all week?"

"Grounded." He looked at the posts mournfully. His rifle was not in its place on the rack. "I forgot my rifle," he lied, "and I didn't bring anything to shoot at."

"What was it you tried to steal?"

"A photo… in a frame."

Ginny's eyes widened. She stepped close, reaching into her pocket. "I pulled this out of the trash." She pulled out a wad of paper and unfolded it. Blood rushed into

Thatch's face as she held the wedding photo out to him. "You can use my rifle."

December, 1975

Age 13

Thatch could not feel his toes in his boots. He had sloshed water filling the horses' trough, but he was reluctant to go inside to change his socks. Jed had developed a habit of coming into Thatch's room earlier than necessary. He didn't even bother to wake Thatch before climbing into his bed. The boy woke to cold hands and pain. This morning, he had slipped out of the house before Jed could blunder in, and got straight to work with the hope his productivity would deter any advances.

The stable was quiet except for the shovel scraping the ground. Urine and spilled water made the straw freeze to the floor, and Thatch's muscles burned from the additional effort it took to muck out each stall. Despite this, he was calm; His mind always grew blissfully clear during hard work. He had found a way to elude Jed, at least in the mornings: His uncle never dared to use him in the stable, where the ranch hands might catch him. He hoped this would still be the case, although he and Virgil were the only ranch hands left–and Virgil didn't come in until later.

The scraping of boots made his stomach drop. He frowned, but forced himself not to turn, to continue shoveling shit. He carried it to a pile by the gate. A brawny arm wrapped around his neck and pulled him against his body. Jed still towered over his nephew, who stood just under six feet. Thatch's throat tightened as he felt his uncle's erection jabbing him. His first impulse was to sigh in resignation, but in a burst of energy, he jerked out of Jed's grasp.

"I'm not done yet." He tipped the empty shovel over the pile as if it had manure clinging to it. The muscles in his shoulders were as tight as twisted wire. He could imagine his uncle's dumbfounded expression, the red rage rising up his neck, into his face.

Just swing the shovel. Just swing the shovel. Take his head right off.

Thatch anticipated being pulled back or twisted around. He did not expect it when he pitched forward. Jed shoved him, tearing the shovel from his hands. Thatch fell face-first into the pile of waste. Shit filled his nose. Moldy, urine-crusted straw stabbed his face. He pushed himself up, retching. Jed shoved his face back down with a boot. Waste, straw, and anything else found on the floor of a stall filled his mouth, mixing with vomit. Thatch began to choke on it, to drown in it. He tried in vain to scream and fight, flailing his arms.

Jed grabbed the waist of Thatch's trousers and yanked them down to his knees. He grabbed the boy's shirttail in one hand, his genitals in the other, then dragged him out of the pile. Thatch hurled, evacuating the waste. As his uncle continued to drag him, he clawed at the ground, screaming. The horses began to rear and squeal in panic.

When Jed released him, Thatch rolled onto his back, but his uncle stood stock-still, jaw jutting, eyes fixed on the door.

Virginia Roanhorse stood at the mouth of the stable. Her eyes were wide with fear and confusion. Her chin quivered. Thatch whimpered and pulled his shirttail down over his genitals. The movement drew her eyes from the man to the boy. With a sharp gasp, she shot out of sight.

Jed flexed his fingers, grasping at something invisible. He turned his cold, grey eyes to Thatch. The boy backed away until he hit a gate. Jed's gaze flickered over him hungrily, but he turned away.

"Clean that shit off," he grunted.

As soon as Jed lumbered out of sight, Thatch was overwhelmed by the smell of shit. Twisting over, he vomited until he passed out.

March, 1976

Age 14

Thatch stared at the phone. He was more afraid of it than he was of the wolves that had started prowling the valley. He had only used a phone three times, all at school: when he got food poisoning, when he got into a fight with a group of boys, and when he pretended he had food poisoning again. He never had any friends to call... except Ginny, who had not been back to the ranch since the incident in the stable, and Virgil seemed to be avoiding him.

The Roanhorses' phone number had been scratched into the wall under the phone, above Slope's Valley HS and Corey Harper, Jed's lawyer and financial advisor. Thatch picked up the receiver with a trembling hand. A few of the numbers had worn off the keypad. His mother had painted them back with small, delicate strokes.

"Roanhorse." Even over the phone, Thatch recognized Virgil's voice.

"Is... Is Ginny there?" He hoped he didn't sound rude. Virgil had a *look* he would give when he thought the boy was being rude. Thatch could never tell if he was doing it to joke with him, or if he seriously wanted to wring his neck.

There was a pause. "Thatch?"

"Yeah." He was certain the look just passed over Virgil's face. "I mean, yes."

"No, son, Ginny's not here." Thatch never admitted it, but a warmth flooded his chest whenever Virgil called him "son." He wondered if that was what having a father felt like. "She's running errands with her mother."

To prevent him from hanging up, Thatch blurted, "You know, I just haven't seen her in a while. And... and... I haven't really been able to ask you, either."

"Well, son... it's been a bit"–he sighed–"...a bit of a challenge keeping up with school."

"I can help." He had taught Ginny how to shoot. Surely, he could teach her algebra.

Virgil sighed. "I'm sorry, Thatch. You and your mom are welcome to visit us in town, but Ginny won't be coming back to Flint Ranch."

Thatch felt like the floor had been pulled out from under him. Jed never allowed him to go anywhere alone with his mother. "W–why?" The silence lasted so long, he was afraid for a moment the phone had disconnected. He snatched at words, trying to think of something to say. "Is– is a Red school very different from a White school? Harder?"

"No, son, it's just different."

Thatch breathed a sigh of relief.

"And, son?"

"Yes?"

"Call it that again, and I'll knock you on your ass."

His face flushed. He couldn't believe he said it himself; Jed said it so often, it just slipped out. "Yessir."

February, 1977

Age 15

Virgil Roanhorse quit Flint Ranch. Thatch's eyes widened to see Jed walk in with blood running down his face, a dark line across his nose where it had broken. Jed glared daggers at the boy, daring him to speak, as he limped to the phone. He scratched Virgil's name from the wall. Thatch's heart sank when he realized he didn't know where else to get the number, if he ever wanted to try to call Ginny again.

But that probably wouldn't have happened anyway.

A few days later, Mr. Harper's name had been scratched out. The phone was gone as well. Thatch found pieces of it in the trash can. His workload tripled, as Virgil was gone and Jed had to devote more time poring over his ledgers. He became quiet and aggressive–more so than usual. To Thatch's good fortune, the stress also prevented his uncle from getting an erection.

Thatch had never slept so well.

****

Before Thatch took his seat–front corner of the class, since his surname was Adams–he checked the chair for a wad of gum or a more exotic unpleasantness, like a strip of denim with pins poked through it. Someone had emptied the pencil sharpener on it. Thatch brushed the shavings into his hand, dumped them in the trash, and sat down as if nothing were wrong.

A group of large boys wearing JV jackets milled around the doorway. They talked in raucous voices and forced their female classmates to brush past them. Thatch was grateful he had arrived before them. If he had to walk through them, he would have ended up with a stinging red welt on the back of his neck, or his jeans around his ankles. He pulled out a worn copy of *Foundation* and leaned over it, raising his arm to hide his face from them. He managed to drown out their voices until the bell rang, and they dispersed.

"Isn't that right, Horse?" A sharp elbow dug into his shoulder, knocking him off balance. One of the JV boys, Allen Dancier, jeered down at him as he sat down. "Just say yes," he advised.

"I won't," Thatch replied, rubbing his arm. He had learned long ago, "yes" and "no" were both potentially humiliating answers.

"Sissy," Allen muttered, taking the seat directly behind him.

"Asshole." Thatch held his breath, bracing. But Allen did not retaliate. Not immediately.

Mrs. Knox assigned a chapter in their history books and began to write a list of ancient civilizations on the board. Thatch skimmed the chapter and leaned back, his textbook in his lap with *Foundation* open inside. After five minutes, he heard Allen shifting around in his desk.

"*Pssst!* Hey, Horse."

Thatch ignored him. He re-read the sentence he had been on.

"Horse," Allen hissed a little louder. Maybe if Thatch ignored him longer, he would grow loud enough for the teacher to hear. "Sissy-boy."

Thatch's eyes were now fixed on the same word.

"Ffffffaaaggot…"

Thatch clenched his teeth.

"Allen, may I help you?" Ms. Knox paused in the middle of *Nubian* and turned.

"Just asking for a pencil," Allen replied.

Mrs. Knox wasn't convinced. She stared at him before her eyes slid to Thatch.

"I'm on my last pencil," Thatch said, holding up the three-inch nub that somehow had to last him until summer. At the beginning of the school year, his mother brought him some meager supplies–often second-hand. When they ran out or were stolen, they did not get replaced; Thatch was usually too ashamed to ask for more. He and his mother did not talk anymore anyway.

"I will loan you both pencils when we begin the assignment."

"Thanks, Ms. Knox!"

Thatch blinked at this unexpected generosity, too surprised to express his gratitude. His relief was short-lived: He discovered Allen *did* have a pencil when he started jabbing Thatch's back with the tip. When Thatch did not turn, Allen leaned forward.

"I was sayin' earlier that people who work close to animals–like horses–they're more likely to get venereal disease," Allen whispered. "You know that's true, don't cha, *boy*?"

Despite Thatch's determination to ignore him, his muscles twisted like wires.

"God knows, girls wouldn't keep you company, even if you *did* show interest in 'em…"

Thatch lowered his burning face. He tried to swallow the bitterness that tightened his throat. Why would they notice he didn't harass the girls like they did?

"Maybe your ma keeps you company…" Allen continued.

Thatch's ears tingled with heat. He was certain if he asked to go to the nurse, Mrs. Knox would notice the heat and allow him to leave. But he didn't trust his throat to work properly; If he opened his mouth, he would only croak.

"Personally, I'd take a horse over your ma."

Thatch clenched his fists. His muscles were twisted like charged springs.

"But not a sissy-boy like you... not a *faggot*."

Inhaling slowly, Thatch stared at the woodgrain of his desk, worn and scratched from years of use and vandalism. His skin was so hot, he was certain if he didn't cool down somehow, his brain would boil. Allen fell silent. The tightness in Thatch's throat loosened, but his face remained hot. Sure he would be able to speak now, he raised his hand.

"You know, I hear your uncle's a pretty good-lookin' guy."

Like a spring releasing, Thatch's raised arm swung. The back of his hand caught Allen across the face. Thatch didn't realize what had happened until he was twisted around in his desk, hand throbbing. Allen stared in shock. A bright red splotch spread across his pale face.

"Thaddeus Adams!" Mrs. Knox cried. Thatch deflated. What a way to show his gratitude...

"I–I'm sorry–" he stammered, looking between the teacher's disappointment and Allen's anger. "I didn't–"

With a roar, Allen lurched forward. He grabbed Thatch's shirt and dragged him to the floor. Thatch raised his arms to cover his face. He was surprised at how light Allen was when he sat on him. His blows glanced pathetically off Thatch's arms.

Thatch was accustomed to far worse.

The students surrounded them in a rumble of shouts and scraping desks. Mrs. Knox was screaming beyond them as they chanted: *Fight! Fight! Fight!*

Taking a deep breath, Thatch braced himself against the floor and thrust his fist up. He made contact. Allen fell still. When Thatch peered around his shielding arms, his breath caught in his throat: He thought he had hit him in the shoulder or something, but dark, thick blood flooded down Allen's face, staining the white wool of his JV jacket. His eyes drifted out-of-focus. With a groan, he slid off Thatch's torso and fell sideways.

The classroom fell silent, except for Mrs. Knox sobbing somewhere beyond the crowd. Thatch pulled himself free of Allen's legs, looking around in disbelief. He was surrounded by wide eyes and gaping mouths. Turning, he found several angry, glaring boys in JV jackets. With a gasp, Thatch sprang to his feet and shot toward the door. Rough hands grabbed his arms and dragged him back down.

Thatch and five other boys sat in chairs lining the wall of the front office. Four of them–the four latter assailants–scowled at the secretary as she tapped incessantly on her typewriter, debating whether they could pop Thatch one while she appeared distracted. Allen, who had regained consciousness soon after the fight, sat next to Thatch. A blood-stained tissue was shoved up one nostril, and his nose was significantly flatter than it had been that morning. A deep purple bruise spread under one eye.

Each boy sat low in their chairs, knees far apart, arms crossed over their chests. They formed a line of faces covered in bruises, cuts, scrapes, split lips, busted eyebrows. A sixth boy had been sent directly to the nurse with an almost-detached ear. Thatch, however, looked relaxed: His legs were stretched in front of him, crossed at the ankles, his copy of *Foundation* open in his lap. Only a couple of bruises and a busted knuckle betrayed his involvement.

They had all been suspended for the remainder of the week. One-by-one, angry or distraught parents arrived to collect their student. Thatch didn't notice Jed until he was hovering over him, blocking his light.

"Fightin', huh?" he asked.

"Yeah…" Thatch sighed. Remembering the insult that started the fight in the first place, Thatch felt deflated. Despite the chill in the air, Jed wasn't wearing a shirt under his overalls. Thatch's face did not only burn from humiliation: He might be avoiding the many bullies at school for the remainder of the week, but he would have to deal with the one at home.

"They said you started it." Jed glanced over the other boys. They would not meet his steely eyes. "Who finished it?"

Thatch's face burned. He hid it by leaning to slide his book into his rucksack. "I did."

Allen shifted in his chair, but said nothing.

"Well, there's that," Jed sighed. "C'mon, boy, daylight's wastin'."

With a deep breath, Thatch stood and swung his rucksack over his shoulder. Allen shifted again, shooting him a glance.

"Sorry." It was barely audible.

Thatch paused. He would not have believed he heard it, except Allen looked abashed when their eyes met. Nodding, Thatch replied, almost as quietly, "Me too."

He wasn't really *now*, but he knew he would be by the end of the week.

Allen's father stared daggers at them, entering the office as they left. Thatch's muscles jumped with the urge to leave as quickly as possible, but Jed pulled him to a stop on the sidewalk.

"I know you didn't start no fight. What happened, huh?"

The doors scraped open as Dancier and Allen emerged onto the sidewalk.

Perfect timing... Thatch lowered his head as he replied. "He was makin' fun of Ma, and..." he dropped his voice to a mumble, "... he called me a faggot."

Jed took a deep breath as he raised to his full height. He narrowed his eyes at Allen, who grew pale under his steely gaze. He side-stepped behind his father. "That true?"

"So what if it's true?" Dancier gestured to Thatch. "Your nephew threw the first punch–"

"That was an accident!"

"–and what does it matter what he called him! Look at the kid! He doesn't have a pound of muscle on him!"

Thatch and Jed exchanged a glance. No muscle? How could he haul bales, then? And how does a thing like that make someone a faggot? Thatch drew up to his full height as well, rolling his shoulders back. He didn't look so scrawny now.

Jed looked him up and down. "Go sit in the truck," he growled, then glared at Dancier.

"Go stand by the car," Dancier told Allen.

Now Thatch and Allen exchanged worried glances. Dancier was brawny, but Jed was easily a foot taller. The boys trudged toward the parking lot.

"Is your uncle about to kill my dad?" Allen whispered.

"I don't know," Thatch replied, glancing after them.

As the men walked around to the back of the school, the boys walked to their respective vehicles. Thatch tried to immerse himself in his book, but ended up gazing over to Dancier's car, where Allen sat on the trunk with his chin on his fist. Fewer than ten minutes passed, but it felt like an eternity before Jed and Dancier, side-by-side and moderately scraped-up, walked back across the parking lot.

Jed opened the door and climbed in. He winced as he lowered himself into the seat.

"Who won?"

"Weren't no real winner. Weren't no real fight," he grunted. "I knocked him on his ass and got my point across, huh."

Thatch watched in silence as Allen got into Dancier's sports car and they zoomed away.

"Uncle Jed..." He was concerned about the response to this question, but it crawled out of his mouth as if it had a life of his own. "Why'd you do that for me?"

Jed furrowed his brow, flicking his eyes over his nephew before turning back to the road. "Man called you skinny, huh. That kinda insult to you is an insult to me. Like I don't feed you enough."

Thatch blinked at this leap of logic. He and Judy were often without food; It never bothered Jed as long as he could feed the horses. They sat in silence until Jed pulled in front of the house. He cut the engine. Looking perplexed, he ran a hand over his chin.

"Lady on the phone said there was six boys?"

"Yeah…"

He looked at Thatch askance. "They all look as bad as the other boys sittin' there?"

Thatch pursed his lips, then snorted. "You betcha."

Jed cracked a grin that went all the way up to his eyes. In all of his years, Thatch had never seen it before. His chest swelled with pride.

Three Days Later

The horses were exceptionally skittish. Thatch wrapped his arms around their necks, whispered to them, even sang to them, but they would not calm down. He realized what it was when he found tracks in the mud around the stable. It was the only time he ever disturbed Jed of his own accord: pulling him from the books spread across the dining room table to point to the prints. His throat was so tight, he couldn't even squeeze the word out. A lone wolf could bring down a horse. A pack could destroy the herd, all the friends he had left.

"Get your rifle, boy," Jed ordered.

Cassie was the smallest horse they had. Jed pulled her out, but he didn't saddle her. Although she was skittish by the barn doors, where the wolves gathered at night, she calmed down as they ventured farther out. Jed took her out to the far side of the enclosure, where the three posts were hammered into the ground, and tied her there. He returned to where he had told Thatch to wait by the fence, about twenty yards off.

"Wait, what are you doing?"

"Bait," Jed grunted.

"WHAT?"

Jed did not reply. He raised Thatch's rifle and found Cassie in the scope.

"Stop!" Thatch reached for the barrel, but Jed shoved him back. He didn't raise the rifle again, but leaned it on the fence.

Thatch stared at the mare, swallowing hard. *I should be the one with the rifle*, he thought. He was the one to shoot coyotes, to bring rabbits, squirrels, and deer in when Jed could only afford to feed the horses. But he didn't dare say it aloud.

The sky grew dusky. The harder Thatch fought to stay awake, the more his eyelids drooped. He snapped awake and found Jed nodding off as well. Cassie tugged at her tether, but bent her head to continue grazing around the broken glass on the ground. Thatch bowed his head once more.

Jed grabbed his arm and shook him awake. Thatch turned to find Cassie still milling about on her tether. Listening, he couldn't hear anything but nightbirds. He was about to ask what was wrong, when Jed gestured for him to stand.

"Stand up," he said. "Pull your pants down, huh."

"Wha–*now*? What about–"

Jed rose to his feet. "The fuck did I say, boy?"

Thatch clenched his teeth and stood. Jed shoved him against the fence. Thatch stood still, unwilling to help his uncle as he wrestled with his belt and jeans.

It didn't even hurt anymore.

They were both awake now, waiting, watching, listening. Jed kept the rifle cradled in his arms. Thatch realized this must be a security measure. He had certainly considered snatching it away and ending all of their problems. He was old enough to know he could lie to the police. He and his mother could run Flint Ranch together. Maybe even Virgil would come back.

Cassie stamped, snorted, and tugged at her tether. Thatch and Jed crawled forward and crouched at the base of the fence. Thatch's heart pounded as he skimmed the tree line. He thought he saw movement, but could not be sure; It was darkness against darkness. Jed rested the barrel on the rail. When Cassie could not get away, she turned to them beseechingly.

"She's too close to the fence." Thatch couldn't believe he had not seen it before: A wolf could easily dart from the cover of the woods, take a chunk out of her, and dart back in a matter of seconds.

"Hob."

"But–"

"Hob your lip, boy." Jed glared at him.

"Look out!"

Cassie screamed as two wolves broke from the darkness. She reared back, pulling the tether up over the post. She galloped away with them close on her hooves.

"No!" Thatch screamed. "Shoot!"

Jed pulled the trigger, but the bullet hit the ground a pathetic distance behind the wolves. Four more shadows appeared, joining the charge.

"How could you fucking miss?" Thatch screamed.

Jed was taking too long to line the rifle up. "You didn't sight it in!"

"No, *you* just can't fucking shoot!" Shoving him, Thatch snatched the rifle away. He raised it to his shoulder and proved his uncle wrong by picking off the wolf snapping at Cassie's legs. He turned the bolt and shot the next one. There were still four more. He pulled the bolt, but before he could chamber the round, the rifle was yanked from his hands.

"No! What are you doing?" He was silenced by the butt slamming into his jaw, knocking him back to the ground.

Jed's face twisted with rage. He straddled the boy and began to pummel him. In the distance, Cassie began to scream.

"They're gonna kill her!" Thatch twisted to block Jed's fist and struck back. He had never tried to fight Jed before; His uncle was so much bigger, but the force of the blow knocked him off.

Thatch grabbed the rifle. He flew after the horse's scream. He could see the shadows move across the grass, flashes of nocturnal eyes. Raising the rifle to his shoulder, he paused every few feet until the remaining rounds were spent. He turned the bolt and pulled the trigger uselessly as the remaining wolves ran away.

Cassie was gutted. She lay on her side, crying in pain, attempting pathetically to raise her head. Moonlight glinted off the shining entrails trailing out of her belly. Tears ran down Thatch's face as he dropped to his knees in front of her.

"I'm sorry," he sobbed. "I'm so sorry, Cassie."

The rifle was lifted from the ground by his side. Jed was going to kill him now; Thatch was certain of it. Jed pulled the clip and loaded a single round. Thatch sniffled, then forced himself to become still. He held his breath. Jed chambered the round. But instead of pointing the rifle at Thatch's back, he stepped past the boy.

"No!" Thatch screamed.

Jed put the muzzle to Cassie's head and pulled the trigger. Thatch stared at the dead mare, once his only source of comfort. His breath came out in ragged gasps.

"You can drag her in." Jed began back toward the house. "We can butcher her tomorrow."

Thatch clenched his teeth. He pushed himself to his feet and charged.

Judy Adams sat at the kitchen table. She didn't dare venture out onto the back porch, but she couldn't bring herself to sleep. She jumped when the clock struck two, then again when the rifle went off. Another hour and a half passed before she heard footsteps.

Jed's heavy tread thudded up the porch stairs. Her heart froze. She did not hear anyone with him. When Jed pushed open the door, Judy's hands flew to her mouth. His nose had been flattened, his top lip and chin were crusted with rusty flecks, and his busted eyebrow was still oozing blood down his face.

"What're you starin' at, huh?"

She whimpered as her heart sank. Her eyes filled with tears. When Thatch's light tread echoed behind him, she could not contain a strangled cry of relief. Her eyes drifted back to her brother-in-law. Although her hand concealed her upturned lips, her eyes glinted with a smile.

Her shoulders lurched with a repressed snort. Jed stepped toward her, but when the springs on the storm door creaked, he stormed upstairs.

Thatch hesitated at the threshold, still concealed by the shadows. Judy swallowed. He was alive. Surely however he looked could not inspire any worse despair than what she had just experienced. When he stepped into the dimly-lit kitchen, she sighed. Blood speckled his face under his nose, but he did not look anywhere near as bad as his uncle.

Smiling proudly, she held her arms out to her son. Thatch closed the door behind him. When he stepped closer, his face was grim and set. He passed his mother with only a glance.

****

It was raining. That's what Thatch believed when he rolled over in bed: There was a torrential downpour outside his window. His eyes snapped open when he smelled the smoke.

He stumbled when he jumped out of the bed, smashing his face on the floor. Ignoring the pain and gushing blood, he threw himself at the window. Thatch's entire world was on fire. Everything he loved. He gasped a couple of times, his chest too tight to take in air. When he could finally breathe, he released an earth-shattering scream.

He didn't remember the door, the stairs, or the kitchen. He burst into the cold outside air in a matter of seconds.

"No!" The stable was fully engulfed. The heat made it painful to breathe. The smell of burnt meat and hair turned his stomach. "Archie!" He thought he could hear the desperate screams of a lone horse, but could not convince himself there was anything alive in there.

He ran toward the fire. Arms wrapped around him and threw him to the ground. He looked up to find Jed bending down to pick a gas can back up from where he had dropped it.

The fire caught in Thatch's chest, a choking, white-hot rage. "You?" he bellowed. "You!"

"Hob your lip, boy." Jed turned back toward the house.

"The horses!" Thatch found his feet and staggered after him.

"You'll understand when you're older."

"Fuck you!" he roared. Jed stopped just short of the porch and turned back to the boy. Fear began to creep into Thatch's chest, but he stood his ground.

"What did you say to me–*boy*?"

"Fuck you!" Thatch repeated, his voice low. Then, swallowing his fear, he screamed, "Fuck you!"

Without another word, Jed swung the gas can, catching Thatch in the side of the face and knocking him to the ground. Thatch pressed his palm over the stinging line running up his cheek. He felt his uncle's hands on his shoulders, shoving him onto his back. The smell of gasoline made Thatch dizzy as Jed began to unbuckle his belt.

Thatch swung his fist. It connected just below the man's eye with a sickening crack. Jed staggered to his feet. He circled around, recuperating from the humiliation.

"You son of a bitch..." He dabbed the sore spot where the bone had cracked, then pointed to the fire. "You're about to join your horses."

They charged at one another. Jed grabbed Thatch's collar and slammed his face into his knee. The boy fell to his knees. Jed pulled him up and dragged him toward the stable. Thatch did not resist, his head flopping to one side. They came so close to the fire, the heat dried their sweat-soaked shirts.

Jed swung Thatch back to throw him into the flames. He toppled off-balance when the boy slipped out of his shirt. Darting forward, Thatch shoved his uncle into the blaze. Jed somehow found his feet and staggered back. Screams of agony came from where his face had been. The smell of meat–his uncle's pain–was invigorating. Thatch reared on one leg and shoved him back into the flames with his foot.

Within seconds, he could not distinguish Jed Flint from the rest of the fire.

With the flames heating his back while the cold air chilled his chest, Thatch stumbled back toward the house. His mother knelt on the porch, clutching the railing. Tears streamed down her face. The fire rose back up in his chest. (*She knew the whole time. She let it happen.*) He stared at her. Setting his jaw, he lumbered up the porch stairs.

She looked up at him with fear in her eyes.